For Mackenzie xxx
T.P.

For my pals Joe, She and Sarah
C.F.

2 4 6 8 10 9 7 5 3 1

First published in 2003 in Great Britain by Gullane Children's Books
Published by Sterling Publishing Co., Inc.
387 Park Avenue South, New York, NY 10016
Text © Tasha Pym 2003
Illustrations © Charles Fuge 2003
Distributed in Canada by Sterling Publishing
c/o Canadian Manda Group, One Atlantic Avenue, Suite 105
Toronto, Ontario, Canada M6K 3E7

Printed in China

Sterling ISBN 1-4027-0429-1

It's a Monster Party!

Tasha Pym & Charles Fuge

Sterling Publishing Co., Inc.
New York

Blot and Og stared out across Blogsville.
"Another day," Blot sighed, and they
stared out the window some more.

"I know!" said Og, "Let's have a party!
A real monster party!"
"You need guests to have a party," Blot said gloomily.
"Who would come here? If only something
happened in Blogsville…"

"Like a bright pink sky," Og said, "filled with guitars?
And streamers and hooplas looped over the stars?
With Whojammacallits and Widjammifoos
zooming round on the clouds
playing koogabazoos?"

"Exactly," sighed Blot.
"*Then* guests would come!"

And then they had an idea . . .

They began writing invitations for their party.
The sky will be pink! they wrote, *and filled with guitars!*
Streamers and hooplas will loop over the stars!
Whojammacallits and Widjammifoos will zoom round
on clouds playing koogabazoos.

Blot and Og watched their invitations disappear over Blogsville Mountain.

Far, far away from Blogsville,
as the sun was coming up,
the Chucks got a
strange surprise...

. . . so did the Jloops . . .

. . . the Vrinks . . .

. . .the Twisums. . .

. . .and the Grolligs!
Everyone was
very excited. . .

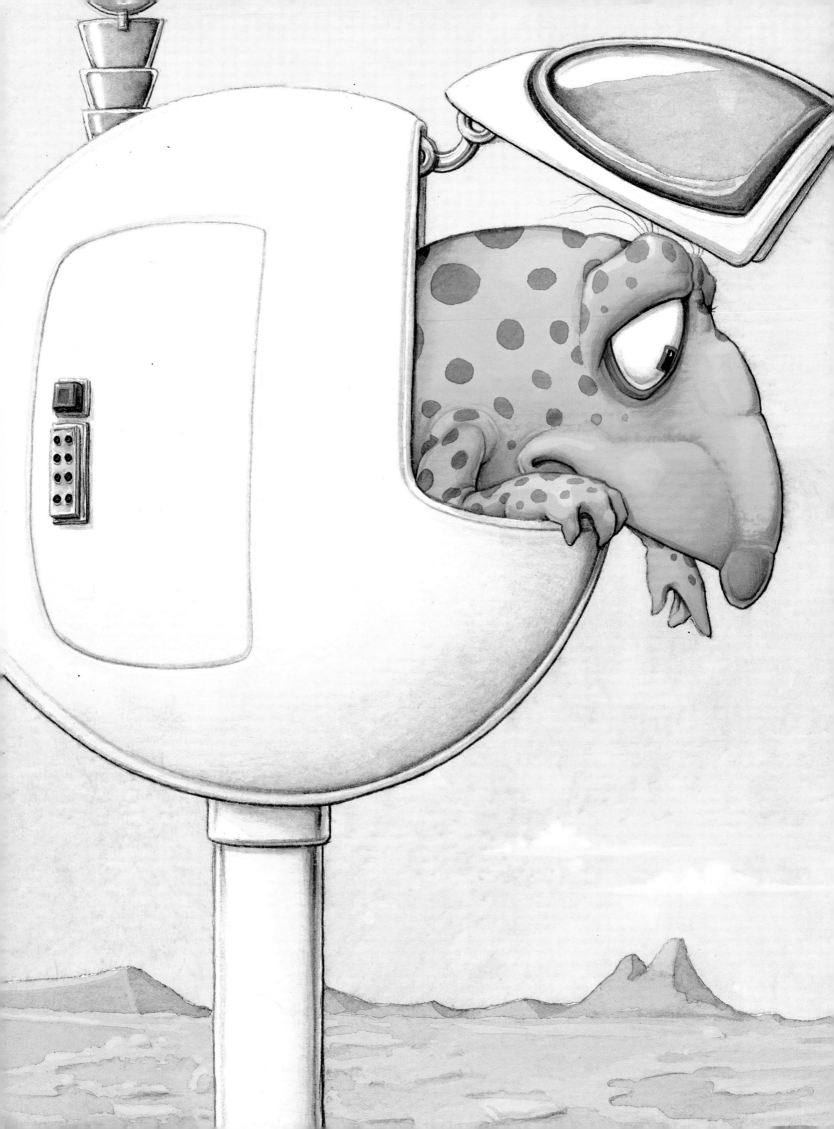

Except in Blogsville.
Blot and Og began to worry.
"What if guests actually come?" said Og.
"We've no pink sky, no koogabazoos,
not a single guitar, not one Widjammifoo!
. . . only this," Og said, and held up a
sad-looking flower.

"Don't worry," said Blot. "They won't come."

But the guests were almost there!

"**Hooray!**" they sang, "for a bright pink sky!"
"**Yippee!**" they laughed, "for guitars that fly!"

"**Whee!**" they cheered, "for hooplas over stars!"
"**Whoopee!**" they cried, "for Widjammifoos!"
"**Wow!**" they yelled, and then . . .

"HUH?!

Where's the pink sky?
The things over the stars?
The koogabazoos?
The flying guitars?
The Whojammacallits?
The Widjammifoos?
You didn't make that up, *did you*?"

But Blot and Og just stared at their guests. They'd never seen so many colors! Or such incredible creatures!

"Who needs a pink sky?" Og suddenly smiled,
"a flying guitar, or a Widjammifoo?
Who needs all those made-up things when
there's Blot and me...

...and all of **YOU?!**"

Everyone looked around.
And, one by one, they began to see
that much more amazing than flying guitars,
hooplas over stars, or koogabazoos...

...would be **making new friends**
and how-do-you-dos!

And then...

. . . the biggest and best
MONSTER PARTY
in the history of
Blogsville began!